pretending with the lumberjack

Hideaway at the Lagoon
Book Two

elsie james

introduction

Welcome to a world where the women are curvy and the men are salivating! Lumberjacks, Ranchers, and Mountain Men are waiting to sweep you off your feet.

Join Elsie's Newsletter and get a FREE EBook

Save big with ebook bundles

Lumberjack Collections
Lumberjack Lagoon
Return to Lumberjack Lagoon
Hideaway at the Lagoon
Lumberjack Lodge
The Buckner Brothers

Rancher Collections
Findlay Farms
Kingridge Ranch
Midnight Kisses at the Ranch

1
kai

My heart thuds in my chest at the feel of Nadia's hands under my shirt. The forest seems to quiet around us. She plants kisses on my stomach and her fingers dance along my zipper.

"Nadia, hold on. It's your turn." I back her against a tree and roam her curves.

She pulls away from me. "Kai, do you want me to check my calendar? I'm sure that it's your turn today. Now come on, it won't take too long for my sister to notice that I'm gone." She pulls me down and I sit on the stump of a massive tree we cut down at work last summer.

Nadia climbs on top of me and her lips press against mine. Her kiss leaves me breathless. Fire ignites between us and rages through every inch of my body. I'm going to miss this when I leave. The weight of her body on my lap has my heart thudding in my chest as she straddles me.

Nadia rocks forward, sandwiching my face between her massive tits and making me pulsate and ache for more. Our mouths collide again and our tongues intertwine in a frenzied dance. Electric sparks shoot through me and I give in to my hunger for her. If she wasn't so damned stubborn, maybe things could be different. Maybe this thing between us wouldn't be temporary.

The cool forest morning and the golden sunrise between the tree canopy disappear. Nadia is all I can see. She reaches between her legs and tugs my zipper down. I give up on trying to maintain my composure. I'm rock hard, my tip is slippery, and she knows exactly what to do.

Her slender fingers wrap around my throbbing length. She pumps with a fiery intensity that sears through me. I thrust into her touch. The rhythmic motion is like a shock wave to my core. Pleasure courses through me and I'm already aching for release.

She slides backward off my lap and drops to her knees in front of me. She spreads my thighs and my breath catches in my throat. This isn't the first time, sneaking off with my new sister-in-law, and my body trembles in anticipation of what's coming.

Her tongue glides down the length of my throbbing shaft, sending shivers of pleasure whipping through me. Nadia looks up at me as she curls her lips around the head of my member. A low groan rips out of me as her warm mouth engulfs me entirely.

She moves her head back and forth, taking me deeper and deeper into the depths of her throat until I hit the back. Nadia hollows her cheeks and it sends me over the edge. My hands instinctively find their way to the back of her head.

Her tongue dances along my girth. She teases me, lingering along the underside of my length. I steady myself from the overwhelming sensations coursing through me, but it's no use. Nadia's every touch consumes me.

As pressure builds in me, I grip a fistful of hair and tug her head to exactly where I need it. I thrust into her mouth desperate for more friction and she gives it to me. With a final bob of her head, my muscles clench and strain. I explode in white-hot bliss and Nadia milks me to the last drop.

I'm left panting, my shoulders thrown back and my chest heaving while Nadia gets to her feet. She brushes the forest floor off the knees of her jeans and I zip up my pants.

"You are incredible." I try to pull her close, but Nadia shrugs away from me. "Hey, I need to tell you something. I'm—"

"Stop it." She cuts me off.

I haven't told Nadia about my move yet. She doesn't know about the apprenticeship or the new life I've worked so hard to create for myself. But there's a part of me that doesn't want to. I don't know whether I'm worried about upsetting her or worried that she won't care at all. Either way, when she cuts me off, I let her.

Her mouth pulls sideways into a smile and she places a hand on her hip. "You can't start looking at me like that if this is going to keep working. Same time next week, right? My turn."

"Yeah, same time." I drop an arm over her shoulder and settle for planting a kiss on the top of her forehead. "But you'll see me later this morning at the bookshop. I've got to meet my brother."

"Can't wait."

2

nadia

I pull the packing slip for the order in front of me and search for the books on our shelves. *The Maid, Things We Hide from the Light,* and *Bath Haus...* I'm pretty sure whoever ordered this could be my new best friend.

Reading has always been my escape. But I never imagined I would work at a bookshop in a tiny lumberjacking town. Especially not one that my sister owns. Hell, I never thought I'd leave our hometown.

If I had to guess I'd have said that by now I'd be a mom and a housewife married to a rancher on some farm. But now I'm a long way from the flat open prairies of Findlay and I've never been happier. Life is funny that way.

Ding. Ding.

The bell on the door chimes and when I look up, my heart flutters in my chest. Kai Greenwood makes a dramatic entrance, not that he has much of a choice. For starters, he's got Buck, the world's most adorable dog, bounding in behind him. On top of that, the man is striking.

He's a massive six foot four inches tall with the muscles of a professional running back. His golden skin is tanned by the sun and his chiseled jawline could cut glass. As much as I try to play it cool, my entire body melts at the sight of him.

I don't blame myself for the swooning. I imagine every woman he comes into contact with feels this way. The fact that I had his dick in my mouth a few short hours ago is technically my fault. But I let myself off the hook for that too on account of being in a sex drought for so long before I moved. Besides, no one else knows about it, so it's like it isn't even happening.

"What's up, Nadia?" Kai's eyes rake up and down my body pulling goosebumps from my arms and a stubborn smile across my lips.

"Good morning." I look up at him through long, dark, lashes not giving anything away. There are worse things than being greeted by a handsome and charming lumberjack this early in the morning.

"Brought you a coffee from Lumberjills, white mocha, extra whip, topped with cacao nibs, and a perfect one-hundred-three degree so it would still be hot by the time I got here."

Ugh, this man is already irresistible, and now he has coffee too. Kai hands the paper cup to me and his fingers linger on mine for a half second too long sending zaps of electricity whipping up and down my body.

"Thank you." I pull my hand away from his and look at my sister, Ariella, out of the corner of my eye.

Kai follows my line of sight and projects his voice. "You haven't changed your mind on that whole, *I'm an independent woman this year* thing, have you? Because I haven't changed my mind about wanting to take you on a date."

And I haven't changed my mind about wanting to lick this coffee off your bare chest but you don't hear me shouting that across this bookshop.

"If anyone could break me, it'd be you. But moving here is my official Eat, Pray, Love moment and I promised myself and my sister three-hundred-sixty-five days of dating me. I'm committed." *There's only three-hundred-twenty-one left, but who's counting?*

"If that isn't the worst thing I've heard all day." A smile tugs at the corners of Kai's full lips.

I let out a soft giggle and remember the tingle of his mouth on mine. The old me would have jumped head first into Kai's massive lumberjacking arms, but the new wiser me is holding space for myself. There will be no more jumping from one relationship to the next.

"Did you come all the way down here to shower me with gifts of coffee or are you looking for a new book?"

"He's looking for my husband." Ariella makes her way towards us.

"I'm right here." Caleb pops his head out of the back office. His voice takes on his typically sarcastic tone. "Our little brother Cain's heading home from his final deployment and this guy thinks we should buy balloons or some shit."

"Party planner of the year right there." Kai chuckles as he and Caleb head for the table in the back of the bookshop.

Ariella picks up a packing slip and we work side by

side. We couldn't be more opposite, but it's easy to see how she fell in love with living here. This bookshop is her life-long dream come true. It's her baby.

She's never wanted the kind you can hold in your arms or the white picket fence that goes with it. Caleb is the perfect man for her and I couldn't be happier that the two of them found each other. Ariella has sacrificed so much for me over the years, she deserves this happily ever after. Maybe I can find mine here too.

Ring. Ring.

3
nadia

Ring. Ring.

I glance at the phone with a half-packed box spilling out of my arms. Then I look at the brass wall clock above it. It's too early for customers to be calling. It's probably going to be another heavy breathing then hang-up call if I had to guess. I head for the phone behind the counter.

Since Ariella left her nightmare of an ex in Findlay, his motorcycle club hasn't missed an opportunity to harass us. It isn't all on Ariella, I've dated a few of the Red Dirt MC brothers too. It was back before I knew better.

Before I left town they were a real concern. They kept tabs on all of us Astor siblings, showing up at our work and driving past our houses. But I haven't worried about it so much since I moved. With the pack of lumberjacks assembled around us out here, Doss and his gang haven't exactly been an issue.

Ring. Ring.

Ariella gets to the phone before I do. "Hideaway at

Lumberjack Lagoon, how can I help you?... It's Ariella Greenwood now, but this is her." Her eyes widen.

I don't miss the way her tone changes and the faint shake of her head. I stare at her watching the subtle changes in her face as she takes the call.

Ariella puts the phone on speaker. "I'm sorry, but this can't be about Nicholas. He passed away three years ago."

Our brother Nicholas' name has me fumbling my books and flying to my sister's side. Doss and his crew have pulled some low blows before, but this is too far. Bringing our brother into whatever this is hits below the belt. Caleb and Kai seem to get it too without my having to say a word. Now all four of us stand in silence, eyes locked on the phone.

The woman on the other line continues in a slow, calculated manner. "Correct, I see that here in the file. To be more specific, this call is about Nicholas' son, your nephew, Tate Astor."

My heart thuds in my chest and I feel dizzy. *What is she talking about? Our brother didn't have a son. He was never given that opportunity because he died too young.* Every muscle in my body tenses.

Ariella blinks, her face washing with a deep crimson. "Who? Wait... what?" She presses a hand to her temple and squeezes her eyes shut.

This is enough. Bringing Nicholas into this and making up a child is cruel. I won't have it. I lean over Ariella, speaking directly into the phone with a tight, clipped tone. "Ma'am, hi. This is Nadia Astor. Our brother didn't have a son."

The woman's voice is kind and gentle. "I'm afraid that

isn't correct. Nadia, my name is Frances and I'm a social worker here in Findlay. Tate is four and he's in my office now. He is entering the foster care system as his mother is unable to care for him. She's signed away her parental rights to the court. I'm contacting you as the next of kin. We need a suitable placement for Tate. If either of you think you might be fit for the position, we'd like to send an agent out to Lumberjack Lagoon and have a conversation."

This knocks the wind out of me. *So it's real. This isn't a cruel prank. Nicholas has a son and he's sitting in a foster care office right now.* I'm too stunned to speak. I can't even see straight.

The room swirls around me and I'm overwhelmed with an intense shockwave of pure joy. *We might have lost Nicholas, but now some stranger is calling to offer us a part of him back into our lives. It's too good to be true.* I'm overwhelmed with an urge to find my nephew, wrap my arms around him, and hold on tight to the last living part of my brother.

France's voice is calm and measured and the sound snaps me back to the present. "Is that a conversation we can have or shall I call down the list? I see you have two additional sisters, Eloise and Roslyn, I—"

"No," Ariella starts, her voice breaking at the end.

My eyes whip to hers. My throat is too dry to communicate all the thoughts whipping back and forth between us. I know parenthood isn't a life Ariella's ever wanted for herself. She just settled into her happily ever after. She gave up her own childhood to raise me and our siblings. But even more than that, I know with everything in me, that little boy is meant to be mine. I can do this. I can give him a life that my brother should've. I don't know what Tate has gone through, but I know I love him.

Ariella inhales into the phone. Her face is drained and colorless and she presses her eyes shut. "I think—"

"I'll do it." I cut her off, my voice vibrating with pure joy. "Start the process, bring him today."

Tears of joy blur my vision. I can't help the enormous grin that stretches across my face. My emotions bubble to surface but I've never been more sure of anything in my life.

"What?" Ariella blinks at me, her jaw falling open.

Frances continues, "I'm pleased to hear that, but Ma'am we can't just send a kid across the country. We'll need to do a home study and make sure the living situation is suitable."

My heart stops for a beat and my throat runs dry. "That's no problem. I'm sure you'll find my home quite suitable for children."

Ariella covers the phone with her hand. Her words hiss out through clenched teeth. "You don't have a home! What are you doing?"

I inhale. "Whatever I have to."

This has to work. It took a million tiny events to bring my nephew to me and I know in my heart that this is the life I was meant to live. Having a piece of our brother back. Being a mother. Being able to hold our family together. It's everything I've ever wanted being dangled in front of me and I'm not going to let it be ripped away.

"Are you sure?" Ariella squeezes my hand and I nod. "Caleb and I will help you every step of the way."

Frances' voice breaks through my concentration.

"Wonderful. We can start the paperwork now if you're available. Your full name please."

My head spins from the whiplash of it all. "Nadia Victoria Astor."

Frances continues, "And your husband's name?"

My husband? Do I need a husband to do this? What year is this? Does not being married make me unfit? No. For sure, no. But what about the fact that I currently live on an air mattress on Ariella's living room floor? That's going to be problematic.

Panic washes over me. I don't want to mess this up. Not when everything I've ever wanted is suddenly within reach. Not when my nephew might be entering the foster care system.

I falter. "Um... I don't, um..." I swallow hard and my vision blurs again. When it comes back into focus, I lock eyes with Kai.

Without a single word, he dashes around the counter and leans over me, speaking directly into the phone. "Kai Greenwood."

4
kai

I grab a rubber band from the cash register and take Nadia's hand. Her eyes are as wide as saucers when she turns to look up at me.

She lowers her voice to a hiss. "What the hell are you doing?"

I pull her hand back toward me and wrap the rubber band around her left finger. "You need a ring. We should do this for real. We should get married."

"What?" Ariella's mouth falls open. She speaks into the phone. "Frances, can you give us a moment, please? We're going to put you on hold for just a moment while we talk logistics. Thanks."

I feel the daggers my brother is shooting at me, but I ignore them. The only person in this room who matters is Nadia. When her eyes meet mine they are wild and unsure. But I'm not. I stare back at her with all the confidence in the world. All of my plans pale in comparison to the prospect of a life and a family with Nadia. If she won't marry me, at least I can sleep at night knowing I helped her get where she was going.

Nadia's words come out through clenched teeth. "Kai, what are you doing? No. No, I don't need you to do this. I am capable on my own. I will figure it out."

"I know you can, but I don't want you to have to. That will make an already difficult situation that much harder. Come on, think about it. We make a great team." I run a charm offensive, pulling out my most smoldering smile. From the way her face is scrunched together, I'd say it gets me absolutely nowhere.

Naida presses a hand to her temple. "Under normal circumstances, I'd be melting into an absolute puddle with that smile, but this isn't the time to be coming undone for a lumberjack who while hot is also apparently insane. We don't even know each other. What are we going to do, pretend to be married?"

"Yes. That's exactly what we do."

Nadia turns to Ariella. "Help me out here?"

Ariella twists a strand of hair between her fingers. "Well, you do live on an air mattress in my living room. That might not paint the best picture of stability. Maybe you let him do it, just for a while."

Nadia's jaw falls open. "What a traitor! Has everyone lost their minds? You want me to run around pretending to be engaged to a lumberjack I hardly know when I am a grown woman. We're losing focus, people. This little boy is our nephew and I know in my heart that I was meant to be his mother.."

"So we'll do this for him." I take the phone from

Ariella. "It's settled. Nadia, we're settled, right? We have to be on the same page if we're going to pull this off."

"Okay," is all she says.

I clear my throat. When I speak on the phone, I don't leave any room for doubt. "Hello, Maam, thank you for waiting. My name is Kai Greenwood and Nadia and I are getting married. It's already in the books... We can't wait to welcome our nephew. Please move forward with the process. Let us know what we need to do and we will have everything ready on our end."

Nadia opens her mouth, but no words come out. Then she covers it with her hand and I wonder what she's holding in. The rest of the conversation passes in a blur as my new reality encroaches in around me.

I know I should be worried, but instead a sense of calm washes over me. In a single phone call, I've become a fiance and maybe even a father. I was made for this. All my life, I've tried to find a path that felt like mine but nothing has ever made sense until I met Nadia.

When we hang up, Nadia puts a hand to her chest and leans against the bookcase behind the counter. I put a protective arm around her and she doesn't push me away. Instead, my chest swells when I feel her fall into the comfort of my arms.

Ariella stares at us in stunned silence. I see a flicker of recognition in her eyes and I wonder if she can see all that exists between Nadia and me. For a few moments, the four of us stand in the quiet of our new reality. The only sound is the chattering of the forest outside.

There isn't any going back now. There won't be a move or

an apprenticeship. Nadia won't get her year of independence. We're in this now, the four of us plus one little boy until death do us part. The faces looking back at me are in varying states of disbelief but this new reality fits me like an old hat.

Finally, my brother breaks the ice. "Kai, what the actual fuck was that."

"Leave it Caleb to say the quiet part out loud," Nadia mumbles under her breath as she pulls away from me.

Caleb folds his arms across his chest. "With all the work you've done, when your life is just about to take a turn... really? This is just like you. How many times are you going to get burned before you stop handing out matches."

"Caleb that's enough." My tone sharpens and I narrow my eyes at him. "I'm not you, thank fucking goodness. I know where my priorities are and I'm acting accordingly."

"What's he talking about?" Nadia looks back and forth between us.

"Caleb, enough," Ariella puts a hand on Caleb's chest. "This isn't up to you."

"It sure as hell isn't." Caleb turns and heads for the door without another word.

"Caleb, I know what I'm doing I'm not—" Before I can finish my thought, Nadia is whipping around to face me.

"It isn't Caleb's fault. He's right. He's the only one keeping a level head about this insane situation. I could've figured it out and you could have stuck to your real life. This is supposed to be my year of being an independent woman dammit and now instead we're supposed to be married and we hardly know each other. Then there's a

little boy who doesn't even know he has this huge family."
I see the tears build behind her eyes.

"Stop it. All of that was before we knew we had a nephew." Ariella says. "Besides, we don't know anything about Tate or what he's been through. He's going to need support from all of us. This changes everything. How could it not? Thank you, Kai. Now I'm going to find that stubborn husband of mine."

5
kai

When it's just Nadia and I left in the bookshop, I put my hands on her arms and turn her to face me.

"Ariella is wrong. Not everything has changed. I've wanted to make your dreams come true from the moment we met. That will always stay the same. Now I have a chance to do that. It isn't exactly the way I pictured a proposal would happen, but I need you to trust me when I tell you, we can do this. You don't have to love me or stay married to me for a lifetime. But we can get your nephew here."

The words hurt as they come out of my mouth, but I mean them. I want the world for Nadia, even if I don't get to be a part of it in the long run. Fire bubbles on my skin where we touch. My chest tightens as I wait for Nadia to decide my fate.

I wish she would stop fighting me. I wish she could see that together we make so much sense. Finally, her eyes meet mine. I see the answer before she says it and I exhale. Nadia shakes her head, but I don't miss the way her mouth pulls up at the corner ever so slightly. I see an unmistakable flush of understanding passing over her face.

"Thank you for being willing to do this. It'd just be long enough to get the placement settled. Once little Tate is here, we can go back to our real lives, right?"

I squeeze her arms and bite back my smile. "Tate is going to be our real life. But we will take it one day at a time. I'm here and I'm not going anywhere until you tell me to."

She chews her bottom lip. "There are so many things I need to know about you if anyone's going to believe we're engaged. I haven't even seen your place. But I already know it's probably better than my mattress on the floor."

"You're going to come over to my place as soon as you leave here and I promise you we will make it all make sense. Can we start there?"

Nadia takes a long inhale. "Yeah, we can do that."

———

I scramble back to my place with just enough time to unpack a few of the moving boxes. If earlier wasn't the time to bring up my impending move, now certainly isn't any better. I've invited Nadia over before, but she's always refused, preferring our secret rendezvous in the forest.

A part of me doesn't believe she's actually going to show up until I hear the tires of Nadia's old Ford Focus crunching up the path toward me. My place still looks like an abandoned shell of a cabin, but it's as good as it's going to be on this short notice.

I open the door before she can knock and Buck bounds

out to greet her. Once he gets his pets from Nadia, I push him aside and pull Nadia into my arms. "Welcome home, sweetie."

Nadia looks stunning, as usual. When she pulls away, she holds up her left hand. When I see the rubber band knotted around her ring finger, I can't help but smile.

"I thought it was fitting for my first visit to our place." She lets out a giggle and I usher her inside. Nadia's eyes widen as they wash over the cabin. "Kai no one is going to believe a woman lives here. In fact, I don't believe that anyone lives here. Are you some kind of minimalism crusader? I mean, where is everything? If it wasn't for Buck's water bowl, I'd swear you were just moving in."

I clear my throat. "Well, what did you expect from a lifelong bachelor, lumberjack-chic? I swear since they renovated that damn lodge in town, everything's gone buffalo-check."

Nadia lets out a long, breathy exhale. "Ha, you have a point. I guess we won't have to fight for space."

"No, we won't. There's a second bedroom down the hall, it's all yours. I'll get you a bed and whatever else you need. This goes without saying, but I hope you'll just share mine." I raise an eyebrow and see her face flush red at the offer.

"Kai, I think we need to take a break from our little hobby. This isn't the time to complicate things."

"You don't want to complicate our fake marriage by having real sex... got it." I let out a chuckle. "Come on, I'll give you a tour."

6
nadia

"I wish my sister were here for this," I call down the hall to Kai. "Who goes on a second honeymoon anyway? They've only been married for three months."

"Why, that means my dumbass brother would be here too and that's the last thing we need today."

"Good point." My stomach clenches and I do one last walk through the cabin. It's only been two weeks since I first stepped foot in here, but it feels like a lifetime. The house itself is unrecognizable. For someone with a tendency toward minimalism, he sure has turned this place into a grand millennial dream.

The white walls are now rich and moody blues and greens. The bare windows are covered with cascading floor-length drapes in gauzy chiffon. The moving boxes that were draped with a tablecloth have been unpacked, finally, and replaced with an actual table. Kai has been the best sport throughout the process.

It isn't just the place that's changed. The sex has faded away between us after I made the request to uncomplicate things. *Do I hate myself for it? Yes. Sometimes. Of course. But was it the right choice? Also yes. Probably. Not sure.*

Though I don't like it, abstinence has somehow made us grow closer. It amazes me the way I've come to depend on him. The man is unflappable in the face of hanging curtains, personal space invasion, and not to mention becoming a fake husband. He's somehow struck a balance between giving me space and making me feel the most secure I've ever been.

Best of all, we've worked together to create the cutest little bedroom for Tate. We spent hours researching the interests of four-year-old boys and the room I'm staying in is fit for a Spiderman-loving, book-reading, lego-playing enthusiast.

"Sweetie, you've got to sit. You're going to burn a hole through that carpet." Kai comes into the living room wearing a button down and I almost forgot how nicely he cleans up.

"I know, I'm just nervous." I look out of the window and Buck comes to stand beside me. She isn't here yet. I scroll through my phone. "Okay, pop quiz." I hold up a photo of my sisters on my phone. "Who are these good-looking ladies?"

Kai examines the pictures. "Those are your younger sisters, Eloise the writer, and... Roslyn who plans on marrying for money."

"Hey!"

"What? You know I'm right. Never met her, but from what you and Ariella say..." He lets out a too-casual chuckle. "Come on, relax. We will be fine. We're completely believable as a couple. This place looks amazing and she'd be crazy not to let us have little Tater over here." Kai squeezes my hand and I find that I believe him.

"You're right. Okay, one more. Give me a quiz."

Kai rolls his eyes. "Who's my best friend?"

"Easy, Garrison, Lumberjack Lagoon sheriff."

Ding Dong.

I hop to my feet. "It's Frances, she's here."

"Before I forget, I got you something. It isn't real, but Ariella told me this would be a nice placeholder." Kai pulls a ring out of his pocket and slips it on my finger. Then he takes a step toward me, puts a hand on the back of my head, and kisses me. His mouth sizzles on mine and my body aches for him. When he pulls away, I stare up at him weak in my knees.

"What was that?"

Kai winks at me. "It's show time." He opens the door. "Frances, hi. Welcome to our home."

Frances comes inside. She's older than I thought she'd be, but she's petite and her body is rock solid. She's stunning without a single swipe of mascara, though she doesn't smile much. There's a real muscle-hamster vibe to her and I'm officially intimidated.

Kai on the other hand doesn't miss a beat.

Before I can think of a single thing to say, he's giving her a tour of our home. Then he tells her a clever story about how we met that has nothing to do with being almost related and having sex in a forest. It's pure lumberjack magic.

Every word out of his mouth is charming Frances, it's written all over her face. But he's charming me too. I'm so grateful to Kai for using his superpowers for good and I feel my heart swell for this man who adores me.

Thanks to Kai's ability to win her over, the home study is off to a fabulous start. An hour after her arrival, Frances feels more like an old friend than a caseworker. She's a Texas native, who instantly fell in love with the forest in our backyard.

That was all the prompting Kai needed. He didn't waste any time taking her out back and showing her how to chop wood. With those massive muscles, she took to the task like a fish to water.

Somewhere between wood chopping and her complimenting my scones, I decide I like Frances. But as we move to the kitchen table to talk business, I can only hope that she likes me too.

Once we're settled in around the kitchen table and I've offered her every beverage under the sun, Frances pulls out her computer.

Frances looks at us over the screen of her laptop as she types. "I shouldn't have an opinion on this, but between me and you, I hope this works out. You are a lovely couple, you have a wedding date on the calendar, and from the sound of it, you've got an excellent support system in place. Little Tate is such a sweet kid. I think it's a wonderful fit."

"Thank you." I glance at Kai and he gives me a reassuring nod, putting his hand over mine.

She continues, "I'm going to need an official statement from you to present to the judge about your plans for the future. It doesn't have to be lengthy, just an idea of where you see your life in a few years."

"Of course. My plan is to get married and be the best mom. I want to keep working for my sister down at the bookshop and give Tate everything." I ignore the fact that this plan is built on a house of lies.

Frances nods along as she types. "Okay, and you Kai. What are your plans?"

"Oh, my plans have changed. I thought I was on a path. But now that Nadia's here I want her to be happy. I want to see her become the mother she's always dreamed of being. I want to take care of my little family."

"Very sweet. Thank you, I'll get this typed up for you."

She isn't wrong. Kai is incredibly sweet, still, a flicker of discomfort passes through me. I wonder what path Kai was on before all of this chaos erupted in front of him.

"So you'll get this wrapped up and we'll have our guy here before you know it then?" Kai's enthusiasm is contagious and I can't help but smile at the thought.

Frances hesitates. "I'm afraid it isn't that simple. Just between us, the placement has been contested by a member of the mother's family. I shouldn't tell you this, but off record, the man petitioning for custody is the child's maternal uncle. Biologically he's got just as many rights to claim Tate as you do. But he's also got strong ties to a motorcycle club. If you can put together a package that showcases your long history of stability, custody is a shoo-in. But they're putting a lot of money behind this, so we have to be careful not to count your chickens before they hatch as they say."

"They don't say that here, I feel like that is very Texas..." Kai mumbles.

My heart sinks. "Is it..." I swallow hard. "Doss? He's in prison, I can't imagine it could be him but..."

"Doss... No, the name is Harvey."

"Harvey." *That son of a bitch.* I think I might be sick. It's Doss' right-hand man. Bile rises in my throat. My head swirls at the thought of my nephew being raised by those jackasses. "So Amber is the mother."

I want to call Ariella, only if I do, she'll talk to Caleb. The last thing I need is Caleb and Kai rounding up a bunch of lumberjacks to confront a motorcycle club. The walls of the room start to close in on me.

"Hey, we'll figure it out." Kai puts a firm hand on my thigh and squeezes.

Frances leans forward and drops her voice to a conspiratorial whisper. "I'm not worried. Let the judge hear your story. Show her pictures of your long history together and this thing will wrap itself up in no time."

"Right." Only we have no history.

7
kai

When Frances leaves, Nadia and I sit at the table and talk things out until she is as pale as a ghost. We go rounds and rounds. But all the talking boils down to two heartbreaking questions from Nadia. *What if it doesn't work and how can I move on knowing that a part of my brother is living inside of that motorcycle club?*

She's spiraling and it's painful to watch. I've gotten to know Nadia so well in such a short time and Tate will be her whole world. That's exactly how I know that she won't be able to sleep unless I intervene. I open a bottle of red and pour her a glass. It takes some convincing but eventually, she has a glass. By the time the second glass is gone, Nadia can hardly keep her eyes open. I take her by the hand and walk her down the hall.

"Come on, there's nothing left for us to do tonight. We will work on this in the morning, but you did a brilliant job with Frances today." I pull back the sheet on Tate's bed and help Nadia in.

Nadia smiles up at me, her eyes glassy from the alcohol. "We both know that was all you. But even with all that charm I don't know if it was enough, I'm worried." She lays back against the pillow and I sit on the edge of her bed.

"I know you are, I am too." I plant a kiss on the back of her hand. "We will figure out a way to get him here. The judge will see it."

Nadia's eyes close and then shoot back open. Her words run together in an adorable slur. "I'm worried about something else too. I'm worried about you. What did you mean when you said you had other plans? Ariella gave up everything for me and I still feel the weight of that. I don't want to take anything from you."

"Ah, don't worry about that. I'd marry you tomorrow and not just because we want Tate here. I'd marry you forever and never look back." But by the time I finish my sentence, Nadia is already fast asleep.

For a minute, I keep my eyes trained on her. I take in the curve of her cheeks and the delicate features of her face. I notice the way her long eyelashes flutter as she drifts off. She is stunning. I want to give her the world because Nadia deserves it. Loving her makes me feel like the man I want to be. I'm desperate to make things right in her world.

When I'm sure she's asleep for the night, I close her door and get to work.

I start by making a call to my brother and interrupting his second honeymoon with the news of the Red Dirt Motorcycle Club's involvement in Tate's life. It takes everything in me not to drive down there and confront these assholes. But I can't make any moves against them with Frances and social services breathing down my neck.

The same can't be said for Caleb. Ever since the Astor sisters have come into our lives, Caleb's been looking for a reason to show them their place in this world. If the situation with Tate goes South, Caleb is the contingency plan I'm not afraid to enact. But I hope it won't come to that.

The next few hours pass in the blink of an eye while I'm making lists, gathering supplies, and charging my camera. I don't sleep, but I don't care when there's so much at stake. I keep my head down and move as quickly as I can.

Before I know it, the sun is up and Nadia makes her way down the hall. She wearing a thin t-shirt with no bra that makes it fucking impossible to forget what her tits feel like on my lips. My body responds to the sight immediately, but I stay focused.

I get my camera ready and snap away as I sing, *"Happy birthday to you, happy birthday to you..."*

Nadia squints into the flash and then sits down at the table in front of the layered cake with an illuminated candle on the top. Her eyebrows furrow in confusion. "Kai, it isn't my birthday and what are you doing up at this hour? It's so early."

"Sweetheart, we're making history today. I know it isn't your birthday. It's not Christmas or Valentine's Day, it's not your graduation. But we're going to celebrate every last one of those events today and document it. We are going to paint a history so stable no judge can ignore it."

Her mouth pulls into a smile. "Kai, you're amazing."

I wrap my arms around her from behind and plant a

kiss on her cheek. We hold the pose while I use my phone to take a birthday selfie.

"We're off to a great start. Now get dressed in your Christmas best sweetheart. The first thing we're doing is heading out back to trim our tree."

Nadia's hesitant smile melts away into a full-blown grin. "I can't wait."

From there, the day is a frenzied whirlwind. We cover all our bases and drive to every corner of Lumberjack Lagoon. Taking pictures where I look like a man in love is the most natural thing in the world.

We pose with coffee and winter hats at Lumberjill's coffee shop. We chase Buck up and down the slide at our local park. Nadia smiles and lets out a giggle when I catch her around the waist and pull her into my arms. We end our night with a romantic Valentine's dinner at Lumberjack Lodge complete with candlelight and off-season heart confetti.

We flip through the pictures on our phones and on my camera. Smiling back at us is a couple in love, that's impossible to fake. Even though I'm running on no sleep, I'm not tired. I'm buzzing with energy. Somehow, Nadia and I share a year's worth of memories in a single day and it leaves me aching for even more time with her. Nadia is without a doubt, my person. I start my truck to get us home.

"You did good, babe. I had so much fun with you today and we have a documented history that no one can contest." Nadia reaches across the center console and entwines my fingers with hers. "Thank you for being you. I couldn't do this with anyone else."

Her touch sends sparks whipping across up and down my arms. "Pretending to love you is the easiest thing I've ever done."

Nadia squeezes my hand. "What do you say we go home and make a night of it... Maybe we can take some pictures you can't send to a judge." She lets out a soft giggle.

"Hell yeah, that's a deal." My dick twitches at the thought of spending a whole night wrapped up with Nadia.

"Oh, Kai, can we make one last stop to get these printed? I want to put them together and get them mailed off as soon as possible. I promise to make it worth your time." She winks and I like where this is heading.

One-hour photo, here we come.

8
nadia

Now my eyes open slowly and even though I'm awake, this still feels like a dream. Golden rays of sunlight filter in through the curtains and bathe Kai's skin in a warm glow. He's still asleep and I trace the outline of his massive arms.

Last night was somehow better than I imagined it would be. Kai and I devoured each other with an insatiable hunger, making up for lost time. My body is drawn to him like a magnet and the anticipation had me losing myself the moment we got through the front door.

This time there wasn't any talk of schedules or whose turn it was. Kai made everything about me. He took his time and peeled every article of clothing off me. Then Kai explored every inch of me with his tongue. I came alive under his touch.

When he couldn't take it anymore, our naked bodies entwined in a frenzy of passion that stretched on for hours. We spent the night locked in each other's fiery embrace. Even when we slept, our limbs were tangled and our hearts beat in perfect rhythm. I thought I'd had every part of him in the forest, but now I understand that he was only getting started.

Kai's peaceful expression isn't disturbed by the sun being up. His steady breaths make my heart flutter with emotion as I replay every minute of last night in my mind. Being in his arms feels like the most natural thing in the world. He's almost too good to be true. But here I am, waking up in his bed.

A rush of adrenaline washes over me when I see the big manilla envelope on his desk. *The pictures, I can't wait to relive the day through pictures. I had no idea he had already taken the time to sort them. I wonder which ones he chose to send to the judge and whether they'll be enough to bring Tate into our lives.*

A surge of euphoria rushes through me as the realization hits that my wildest dreams are within reach. I pull Kai's button-down flannel shirt from the floor and slide it on. It smells woodsy, like him, and I breathe in deeply as I take a seat at his desk.

I run a finger along the folded seal of the envelope. Then I empty the contents onto his desktop. Before I get it open, I'm already grinning because I know what's coming. I'm ready to see yesterday in still shots, but this is something else entirely.

There are copies of Kai's driver's license, the results of a physical assessment and some kind of exam scored with ninety-four-percent at the top. This clearly isn't what I thought. I'm curious, but I remind myself that it probably isn't any of my business.

Kai isn't actually my husband. It shouldn't be a surprise, but somehow It's a bit of a shock when I think about it. I've been so selfish. Kai has had an entire life before me. This is clearly a holdover from that time in his life and an important one.

I slide the documents back into the envelope and wonder where in the world he put those pictures. But as my eyes swipe over the documents, I pause. I can't unsee the typed letter at the bottom of the stack of materials.

Congratulations on your acceptance into our program.

I scan further down. This is an acceptance letter for an apprenticeship and it's dated just a few weeks ago. A pit forms in my stomach. From there I can't help myself, I read it from top to bottom, pouring over every detail.

Dear Kai Greenwood,

Congratulations on your acceptance into the lineman apprenticeship. Based on your exemplary test scores and exceptional pole climbing ability, we are pleased to offer you a spot in our residency program as well as a generous relocation bonus.

Please note that only the top two percent of applicants are accepted Into this prestigious program. You should be proud to find yourself among them. We are certain you will find a career with us that is unmatched.

Pack your things and prepare for a move in the next thirty days. Our relocation specialist will be reaching out to you with more information.

Sincerely,

Brain Chavez,

CEO, Brotherhood of Electrical Engineers

My chest hollows out and then collapses in on itself. I ache with a deep emptiness that leaves me unable to breathe. No wonder his house was packed. I knew he wasn't a minimalism enthusiast!

Kai is putting off a once-in-a-lifetime opportunity for me. He's done all the hard work and he's succeeded. I won't let him give that up. The crushing burden of guilt engulfs me like a tidal wave, dragging me under until I'm suffocating.

This situation with Kai is like my sister all over again. Watching a person I love give up their life for mine is not something I'm prepared to do again. But back then I was a child and I didn't have a choice. Things are different now.

Bringing Tate into my life is my dream. This apprenticeship is Kai's and I won't be the person who takes this from him. I take action immediately, springing to my feet and moving in silence collecting my belongings from his bedroom.

Kai is too sweet, too kind and he deserves to have everything he's ever wanted. I need to fix this, but I know him so well. He won't walk away from me and I love that about him. But it's time I let go of the fantasy of being a family and start acting on what's best for all of us, Kai included.

I pack most of my belongings and scribble a note. We can talk about this later, but after all he did for me yesterday, he deserves a little more peaceful sleep.

9
kai

My arms reach out for her before my eyes open. I want to feel her warm curves against my hard lines. I don't know what time it is, but sleeping with Nadia's body tucked into mine soothes me like a missing piece to a puzzle that I didn't even know was gone.

My body is still buzzing with the lingering sensations from the most incredible night of sex I've ever experienced. Every touch, every kiss, every moan plays in my mind on repeat. I let my eyes close again and doze off with the memory.

It's another hour before I'm jolted awake by the realization of the empty space where Nadia should be lying next to me. But when my hands make their way over, her side of the bed is cold. I wonder how long she lay awake this morning waiting for me to get up. I wonder what time it is.

I get to my feet and head for the shower. The hot water rushes over me and I can't help but relive every minute of last night. I've never been so captivated by anyone. It is impossible to think when all the blood in my body is concentrated in my swollen member.

I squeeze and stroke, letting myself imagine the swell of her tits, the round of her mouth wrapped around my length, and the way her ass looked tilted up into the air. Nadia is all I'll ever need. It doesn't take me long to explode in white-hot bliss from the thought.

By the time I get dressed, I'm feeling better. I don't see the white piece of paper with my name written on it until I step into the kitchen. But when I do, it pulls a smile from my lips. There's no doubt that it's written in Nadia's perfect calligraphy. Normally surprising her is my thing, but there is an undeniable charm to waking up to a love letter.

I pour myself a cup of coffee and unfold the paper. But when I read it, my initial surprise quickly transforms into a deep sense of devastation.

Kai,

I want you to know that I have fallen in love with you. You are an incredible man and you deserve the whole world. That's why I've made a decision. I want you to make your dreams come true. I saw your apprenticeship letter and you have to take it.

I'm going to take some time too. I'll be staying at Ariella's place for a few days while she's still gone. Let's respect each other by giving us some space to breathe. Please don't contact me. In fact, I'm going to turn my phone off.

Instead, get things in order to leave for your apprenticeship. I know it isn't too late to make your dream come true, I saw the date. I'm going to figure out what to tell Frances. I think I'll start with the truth, but I need time. Thank you for being my favorite person.

Xoxo, Nadia

The weight on my chest feels like a concrete block. Each sentence pierces my heart with more intensity than the last. The room feels emptier than ever before, and my emotions swirl like a storm inside me. It's taken me all my life to find my place but I know for sure that it's right beside Nadia.

"Buck, your mom's lost her mind on us. She's left us with this terrible fucking plan, but at least she loves me."

Buck puts his head on my lap as I read the letter over and over until I come to a simple conclusion. *I'm not going to respect her space.* I tried that. We lived three months sneaking off to have sex in the woods when we could have been making a history that we didn't have to manufacture. I refuse to stand idle and watch the most incredible person slip away from my life I'm done with following Nadia's plans. It's time to go after my dream.

10
nadia

The next seventy-two hours pass like molasses in January. I sleep as much as I can, which as it turns out, isn't much. I read three books cover to cover, and I exclusively eat bags of gummy candy. None of it helps.

I don't know what I'm going to tell Frances that won't make me look unstable and I sure as hell can't stop missing Kai. This is just like me, I jump headfirst into relationships then sink before I can learn to swim. The most ironic part is that I finally chose the right guy this time only to figure out that I actually am the problem.

But at least the timing of moving-gate has coincided with my sister and Caelb being out of town. I take advantage of the fact that their place is all but abandoned right now. In exchange for the hospitality they don't know they're providing me, I commit to spending extra time popping into the bookshop and packing up online orders to keep things running. It's just about the only productive thing I can do right now.

I walk out to the quaint bookshop behind Ariella's

house and shove the creaky wooden doors. I tell myself I'm making the right choices, but I can't stop my shoulders from sagging with defeat and my eyes from burning with tears as I think back to the disappointment he must have felt as I selfishly ripped open his already-packed moving boxes. Of course, he could have mentioned that he was leaving to fulfill some lifelong goal, but I digress.

Ripping open another bag of sour gummy worms, I turn on Taylor Swift's *Folklore* on vinyl. I'm pretty sure I do feel something like an old cardigan, so it feels right. I throw myself into the online orders.

While I work, I squash down the searing pain that grips my chest and crushes my heart. My entire year of independence shatters into a million pieces as I sit here, reduced to a sniveling mess. Which is ironically the exact outcome I was trying to avoid.

Ding.

The bell chimes against the door as it flies open. Even though he's respecting a boundary I set, a part of me hopes it will be Kai ready to rush in and tell me he loves me all over again. But instead, I see a tanned and smiling Ariella rushing toward me.

What the hell? What day is it? How long have I been under a blanket?

"What happened? I saw the blankets on the couch and I know that look." Ariella comes for me with a big smile. She looks refreshed and glowy. I can only imagine what I look like in comparison.

"Nothing happened. What happened to you? You're back early."

She flips on the electric kettle. "Something um.. Something important came up. But why don't we start with why there's a massive stack of empty gummy worm wrappers scattered through the house."

"Well, it's because I didn't think you'd be home any time soon." I try to blow her off, but when Ariella tilts her head and crosses her arms, I fold. My trembling lips part and I tell her everything. I don't miss a single detail and I don't even try to stop the tears from falling as we talk.

Ariella pours each of us a cup of tea. "Why are you so devastated by the idea of him changing his dream to include you?"

"Because... that's what you had to do. You didn't get a choice. Mom and Dad died and you became a parent. I know what a sacrifice you made for me, Roslyn, and Eloise, even if they couldn't see it at the time, I did. I can't have another person I love making that kind of decision because of me."

Ariella's face pinches into tight lines. Then she comes around the corner, arms open. She wraps me in a massive hug. "Is that what you think? That breaks my heart. You are so... wrong."

"Wrong?" I let out a giggle through my tears.

Ariella pulls back and looks into my eyes, taking her hands in mine. "I never gave up my life for you, I had a life because of you, and I'd do it over a thousand times over. We didn't have parents anymore, my sisters were the only thing tying me to this world. I would've been so lost without you. Now you have a chance to be happy with an amazing man. Don't you dare let that stand in the way."

The knot over my chest loosens and I inhale for the first time since I saw Kai's acceptance letter.

"Do you think he feels the same way?"

Ariella swipes at her own tears. "Are you kidding me? Have you met the Greenwood men? They don't do anything they don't want to do. If Kai told you that he's made a decision to be involved in your life, then he's made a decision. The only thing standing in his way is... you."

"Now that sounds right. It's not the first time I've been my own problem. Ugh, I thought I'd outgrown this." I let out a humorless chuckle. "What the hell am I thinking? I need to fix things with him."

Ding.

The sound of the silver bell against the old door has me whipping my head up. My heartbeat picks up. *It's Kai. I already know it.* My breath catches in my throat and I get ready to throw my arms around his neck.

But my heart nearly stops altogether when I see Frances walk through the front door.

11
nadia

I lower my voice. "Shit. This is the last thing I need right now."

"She's early," Ariella mumbles.

"Early? I didn't know we were expecting her at all."

"Don't worry, I've got this. Go wash your face." Ariella steps around the counter and rushes to greet Frances at the door. "Frances, hi…"

I step into the bathroom, taking the opportunity to collect myself. Checking the mirror I dab the blots of mascara from under my eyes and smooth my hair back into a ponytail. I don't need Frances seeing me in my hot-mess-express era. It isn't going to help my case. Plus, I need to talk to Kai before I put my foot in my mouth with Frances.

Thank goodness Ariella is back and on my side. When I make my way onto the bookshop floor. Ariella and Frances are chatting like old friends and sipping tea.

"Frances, hi. It's nice to see you again. Are you here for another interview or an inspection?"

Frances' eyebrows furrow and she tilts her head to one side. "No, not today. Of course not."

I put a hand on my hip. "So you flew all the way out to Lumberjack Lagoon for... another case?"

Frances looks at me like I'm insane. After a long pause she says, I'm here for your wedding. I thought it was so sweet of you to invite me and I had such a nice visit last time, I jumped at the opportunity to come again. I can't wait to take these photos of the ceremony back with me and include them in your file. Those Red Dirt MC guys don't stand a chance at taking little Tate."

My jaw falls open as I try to process what she's saying. I come up with a few options. Either Frances is batty and making things up or maybe I slept through some kind of alternate ending to my story with Kai. Somehow, Ariella doesn't seem to be confused at all which makes me think the latter is more likely.

Ding.

The bell chimes again, and this time it's Kai. The man is a sight for sore eyes. All I want to do is fall into his arms and tell him that if he moves, I'll move with him. With Frances' eyes on me, I keep myself together and calmly step around the counter toward him.

"Kai, good to see you. Look, Frances is here."

"Frances, hi." He steps toward her, wrapping her in a hug. She didn't strike me as a hugger, but she doesn't seem to mind it coming from Kai. "Thanks for coming."

Ariella gets to her feet. "I have an idea, why don't I take you to your seat and we'll let Nadia get ready."

"Absolutely." Frances holds out her arm and Ariella

slips an elbow through it as they make their way toward the door.

Okay, everyone has officially lost it. I stand staring, my jaw hanging open in total shock.

Ariella turns back to look at me over her shoulder with glassy eyes. "Congratulations, I know this is going to be the best day of your life."

When it's just Kai and me, I look up at him, desperate to make things right. But before I can get in a single word, he puts his arms around me.

"I missed you and your plan sucks. So I came up with my own." He plants a kiss on the top of my head. "We're not going to solve anything by being half in. I love you Nadia and I'm doing exactly what you asked me to do. I'm making my dreams come true. You are my whole world. I'd give up everything if it means getting to love you day in and day out."

"I love you, Kai. You are too good to be true and I'm sorry I almost let my past get in the way of our future. I missed you so much. I don't want to be away from you, ever. I want to marry you, not just for Tate, but forever."

Kai's mouth lands on mine in a kiss that sizzles through my whole body. His hands lock around my waist and I feel him exhale.

"I'm glad you said that because there's a whole wedding waiting for us outside. Ariella helped me pull it together. She's got a dress for you too, it's in her closet. She said it will be obvious. I wanted to bring Frances into the magic of our love story because it's real. I get to marry you and it won't be just us, I get to be a dad to Tate, I know it. The only thing I can't figure out is how the hell a guy like me got so lucky. You are my favorite person, I'll meet you outside when you're ready."

———

As I emerge from the threshold holding a bouquet of wildflowers picked from the forest and wearing my white gown, I feel weightless. The air is filled with anticipation and the excitement is palpable. Twinkling lights dangle from the trees around us, casting an enchanted glow on the forest.

The entire Greenwood family is present and Kai's best friend Garrison is here too. When I see my sisters seated on rows of elegant gold chiavari chairs I smile through blurry eyes. This is a dream. It's too perfect to be real, yet here I am.

My eyes drift up the aisle to the man waiting for me. Kai is blinking back tears as his gaze locks on me. A sense of calm washes over me. I know without a doubt that I will love Kai forever. He's the man I've been searching for and now that we've found each other, I'm never letting go.

12

epilogue: nadia

With trembling hands, I reach out and grasp Kai's fingers tightly. "Oh my gosh," I whisper, hardly able to contain my excitement. "Look, that's him. That has to be him." I can't believe this moment is finally happening. My entire body tingles with anticipation and I'm barely holding onto the emotions firing through me.

My heart pounds in my chest as I stare at the boy in the distance. There's something familiar about him. He's only five but Tate stands tall and proud, just like my brother did.

Frances comes back to her desk, she's hardly able to contain her smile. "Mr. and Mrs. Greenwood, it's my pleasure to introduce you to Tate. He's the coolest kid I've ever met and I'm thrilled that he'll be going home with you today."

Tate steps out from behind her and it's surreal. It's like looking into the past. There isn't any doubt that this little guy is an Astor. He's got the dark hair, the striking eyes, and the same deep-set dimples that my brother had. He looks up at me and time stands still. Every memory I have of my brother growing up floods back to me.

With a shaky breath, I hold out my hand to him. "It's nice to meet you, Tate. I'm really happy you're going to move in with us. I'm Nadia, your Dad was my little brother. "

"I know." He shoves his hands in his pockets.

My voice wobbles and I hold back all the things I want to say. *I'm sorry you've ended up here. You are loved. You are going to be okay in this world because we are going to make sure of it.* I can't imagine what he's been through.

"You know back home, we have a room all set up for you. I brought you some pictures of it, just in case you want to see them." I hand him my phone and he flips through the photos.

"That looks cool, so many trees there." The ghost of a smile plays on his lips and he pushes his hair away from his eyes. His arms fold tightly across his chest and when he sits in the chair next to Frances' desk, his shoulders sag.

"Tate, is there anything you want Nadia and Kai to know about you? Maybe you can tell them a little more about what you like to do or how you're so good in school."

Tate looks around the room and then inhales. "I just want to say thank you for, you know, wanting me to come with you."

The floodgates burst open. My heart breaks for what his little life must have held so far. "We want you so badly. I loved you from the moment I heard your name. I know it will take time, but I think that you'll find out we're pretty cool." I swallow my tears and Kai plants a kiss on the back of my hand.

"Yeah," Tate nods.

Frances opens a folder and lines the table with documents. Together they paint a clearer picture of Tate's past, but I can't keep my mind off the present. I want to know everything about this kid, but he shouldn't have to relive whatever is written on those pages.

"I, uh, I don't know if we should…" I start.

Frances looks at me, eyebrows arched. She may have missed my point entirely, but Kai gets it.

He leans forward with one eyebrow arched. "Hey Tate, I heard that you think you're a pretty fast runner in your new shoes… I bet I can beat you."

"He's kidding. Tate, you'll get to know us, he's joking with you." I clench my teeth and cut my eyes at Kai. "What are you—" I start, but then I stop when I see Tate's posture change.

Tate bolts upright. "I'm super fast!" A slow-growing smile stretches across his face and the sight brings tears to my eyes.

Kai jumps to his feet and gives Tate a head nod. "Are you ready to prove it or what? Let's get outside, it's so boring in here. I'll tell you what we'll race and the winner gets ice cream before we head back to the airport."

"Yeah," Tate looks like a child for the first time since we met him. His eyes light up and he looks from Frances to me and back again, "Can I go?"

"Of course you can," I say.

"We'll leave you to it. We've got to figure out who's faster, right Tater?" Kai holds up his massive hand and Tate gives him a high-five.

Kai bounds out of the back door of the social services

office with Tate trailing close behind. As I watch them walk, my heart explodes with joy. I don't know whether it's my imagination, but I swear that Tate copies Kai's stride.

Frances steps away to grab another file and my phone vibrates in my pocket.

Ariella: Can we come over to meet him yet?! Are you on the plane at least? What's happening over there?

Me: All my dreams are coming true. You and Caleb will be the first to know when we touch down!

Ariella: Me, Caleb... and Eloise. She's here.

Me: Holy shit.

how to lose a lumberjack in one date

When Ariella Astor found herself hiding from a motorcycle club in Lumberjack Lagoon, she discovered more than just a safe place. She found Caleb Greenwood, her other half. He's a man who loved her so hard, she stayed forever.

Her sister Nadia Astor was short to follow. When she arrived at the lagoon, she had more than just a new town to explore. A phone call led to the discovery of a child who could be all hers... There was only one problem: she couldn't do it alone. Caleb's brother Kai was quick to step up, and the rest, as they say, is history.

But there are more Astor and Greenwood siblings floating around. When Eloise Astor came into town at the same time Cain Greenwood was home from deployment, Ariella and Nadia cooked up a plan.

What if the third Greenwood brother and the third Astor sister became a thing? What if they got together only to find they couldn't resist each other? It would all be so very-Brady-wedding magical!

Spoiler alert... That isn't what happened. Before you read Eloise's story in Single Dad Lumberjack or Cain's story in Captivated by the Lumberjack, I think you need to experience this date gone wrong.

This is how you lose a lumberjack in one date...

eloise astor

Ugh. If this dude looks at his phone one more time while I'm talking, I'm walking out of here. I don't even know exactly where *here* is, but I'm not a fan. This is some sort of adult Chuck-E-Cheese, only designed especially for Lumberjacks.

I'm all for cheap beer and pool tables on a first date. But with the axe throwing and the buffalo check tablecloths, this place is on a whole new level. I finish off my beer, and then I clear my throat with extra emphasis. It's a not-so-subtle warning shot of sorts, and I hope my blind-date lumberjack will take the hint. After all, Cain Greenwood isn't bad to look at.

Don't get me wrong, he's definitely got a lumberjack vibe... even his name screams *Man of the Forest*. But I suppose that comes with the territory. With his chiseled jawline and blinding smile, I could be convinced to climb him if the situation presented itself.

The waitress takes our order of mozzarella sticks for

him and more beer for me. I don't miss the way she throws her hair back and bats her eyelashes at Cain. I can't help but think they might make a nice couple. I even find myself subconsciously wishing her luck, which isn't a great sign for him and me.

Cain doesn't seem to notice her at all. When she vanishes, he offers me a casual glance from over the top of his beer bottle. His phone is still in hand and that's all it takes for me to decide that I'm over it.

I throw in the towel right then and there, determined to call it as I see it. "So, you're back from deployment and already busy, huh? Lots of people to text right this minute it seems…" I trail off with a shake of my head.

Cain Greenwood meets my eyes for what can only be considered a half-second and nods. "Yeah, it's an old friend. Sorry, I just need a minute. I know this is rude, I wouldn't normally, but this is important. Let me step away… I'll be right back."

"You know what? I'm not worried about it, take all the time you need." I shrug and am surprised to find I really mean it.

I've never been someone who needs company. When that company is looking longingly at a text message, I'd much rather be alone. As soon as he leaves, I finish my beer and then I finish his too. Just like that, I'm feeling better about the night. Not better like *maybe Cain is the love of my life*, but better like, *I just noticed there are nachos on the menu.*

I get my phone out and stare at the blank notes app. Stupid writer's block still plagues me, and that's not great when you write to pay the bills. By the time he makes it back inside, I still don't have any words down. But I do have a nice new buzz that takes the edge off. So I count it as a win.

Cain slides back into the booth. "Sorry about that."

I shrug with a laugh. "Don't worry about it. This is a weird setup, right? Basically, our siblings were like, *hey, you both have dead brothers, so you should go out.* And like, that's just not sexy." I bite back a laugh, but Cain doesn't follow suit.

Instead, his eyes widen. "Are you feeling okay?"

I sit up a bit straighter and reach for the water. "Yes, I'm fine." And I am fine. I'm fine with this being a bad date. But I don't need to get so sloppy he's got to carry me out of here.

He softens, "But I do know what you mean. I can't believe I'm doing this. A blind date isn't my style. But I've been out of practice during deployment, so I guess they thought I could use some help."

I let out a laugh. "Yeah, Ariella hit me with the, *come on we'll be three sisters dating three brothers. It'll be so cute.* But you know, cute isn't my thing. I should've said no straight out of the gate."

"Ouch." A smile tugs at the corner of his mouth.

"I mean... no offense. The night is still young, maybe this will turn around for us." My stomach sinks and I bite my tongue. "It's just that I came here to work on my newest book, not to date anyone. I thought Lumberjack Lagoon would be a good backdrop for some inspiration."

"Oh, so you write romance then?" He leans forward, interest finally piqued.

"No, I write thrillers actually. There are lots of dead bodies and such."

"Wow." He gives an exaggerated nod. "Yeah, okay. I wonder what's taking so long with those mozzarella sticks."

caleb greenwood

The food arrives and we dig in. Thank fucking god the atmosphere lightens as I start to match Eloise drink for drink. But no matter how much I try to talk myself into this, something isn't working between us.

There are facts here that are hard to dispute. Eloise seems cool. She's hot, that's a given. Massive tits, which is a total plus. But I feel like I'd rather high-five her over a keg than bend her over a couch. With as long as it's been since I've been laid, that's really saying something.

I can't tell if it's the hard edge to her that's turning me off or the string of text messages that have my phone vibrating in my pocket. But either way, time is standing still on this date in the worst possible way.

I shake away my thoughts and try to get my head back in the game. "So tell me about yourself. We're technically family now, right? I should know *something* about you other than the fact you write horror stories for fun."

"Ah, there's nothing like a reminder that our family

tree is looking more like a straight line these days. Should we take these shots first?"

"Absolutely." She throws hers back like a fucking pro and I'm impressed.

She might be the perfect woman, but for some reason, I can't make myself feel a single thing.

"So you aren't into scary books?" She teases me, and her mouth pulls up at the corner, her words slurring at the ends just a little.

"I don't know, it's just that I've seen a lot of real-life horror since I've been enlisted. It makes it a little less fun to explore in my downtime."

Fuck. I'm such a drag and I can't get out of my own way.

"Right. Yes... Um, thank you for your service." She tucks a strand of hair behind her ear and stiffens.

I consider ordering another round, but a boy runs past our table. He's got a throwing axe in hand, and I let out a laugh. "Only in Lumberjack Lagoon is a ten-year-old running past you with an axe, not a problem. You know I've always wanted kids. I think they have a way of lighting up a room. There's so much hope in them. What about you?"

Even buzzed, I know that this has got to be safe territory. I mean, everyone likes kids, even if they don't have them or don't want them. Everyone has at least one amazing kid in their life.

She lets out a deep exhale and rolls her neck from side to side. "Yeah, kids aren't really my thing."

"Right, cool."

My phone buzzes in my pocket again. It's Gabby again,

I know it. I know I should be paying attention to Eloise, but I can't help but check the message. When my brother Kameron passed, he left behind too many things to count. But none as important as Gabby.

eloise astor

By the time we've finished eating, we've both stopped trying altogether. But Cain is a gentleman and tells me that he's going to make sure I get an Uber ride home. He needs one too at this point.

The only problem is, there's apparently just one, solitary Uber driver in this godforsaken town. The dude is making his way back from the Portland airport. When I asked how long it'd be, Cain said it was impossible to know.

In lumberjack land, you don't use an app like the rest of America. You simply *text the dude*. He must not anticipate a ride anytime soon, though, because Cain decides that we should play a drinking game. Now that I'm matching him shot for shot, I'm liking him a whole lot better.

As the night wears on, the place goes from a lumberjack amusement park to a dive bar, and I like it a whole lot more. I'm leaning against Cain to keep from falling over in an oversized booth back in a dark corner.

Dammit, he's handsome.

I run my nose up the side of his neck, breathing in the warm smell of leather. When my eyes meet his, I smile. "Can I be honest with you? I wanted this to work so much. Because you're fucking hot and your a lumberjack and a solider at that. You smell so good... But it's a miss, isn't it?"

He lets out a deep belly laugh. "It's a fucking miss! I'm glad you said it."

I can't help but join in the laughter. "Okay, okay, I have an idea. Now we're gonna have to see each other at every family thing from now on since we're technically, and not in a weird way, related."

"True story." He raises his glass in a toast to me.

"So let's just try this to put the theory to bed once and for all. Are you in?"

"I'm so in, Baby." He growls, biting his bottom lip, and winks at me.

He's smooth. There are not too many men who could pull off a sentence like that, and all the women around us seem to take notice. I should feel... something. But instead, I let out a giggle.

"Okay, Daddy, give me your hands," I purr.

I take Cain's hands and use them to cup my breasts. I press them together, leaning into him and crawling onto his lap. I straddle him, rocking up against him before I plant my lips on his.

He runs his hands down my back and settles them on my waist. When he parts his lips, I slip my tongue inside. I take my time, exploring every corner of his mouth. My fingers dig into his scalp.

When I pull away, I stare into his eyes. I give him my sexiest smile as I say, "Sorry, Babe, nothing."

"Not a damn thing." He laughs and smacks my ass as I climb off of his lap. "What the hell is wrong with us?"

I let out an easy laugh, shaking my head. "I have no idea, but I don't think either of us is getting any tonight."

"Maybe not, but I sure as hell want to beat you over at the pool table. Get up, let's go."

I raise an eyebrow at him. "You've challenged the wrong drunk girl. You're on."

———

A half-hour into our game, Cain steps away to use the bathroom, leaving his phone on the side of the pool table. When it vibrates, I can't help but look at the screen.

Gabby: Are you going to stop by after your date?

Now that's interesting. *Who are you, Gabby, and why would you both know that he's on a date and be asking him to stop by at this hour?*

When Cain reappears, he grabs his phone from the side of the pool table. "I thought I was going crazy, couldn't figure out where I left this." He opens it, and I see a flicker in his eyes as he reads the message. "Hey, uh, I've got to run. I'll call for the Uber again..."

"Don't worry about it. I'm sober, I can wait. You should go." *Gabby, whoever you are, I've got your back, girl.*

"Are you sure?"

"Yeah. Have a good night, Cain."

"You too." For the first time all night, light fills in the shadows under his eyes.

He hugs me and pays our tab in full. Cain may not be my person, but as a brother-in-law for my sisters, he's top-notch. Gabby has herself a good man right there. His exit is dramatic, a swift leap toward the open door, and just like that, he disappears into the wooded area out front like a lumberjack Jacob-freaking-black.

All of a sudden, I feel a rush of inspiration. I pull out my phone and punch out the first draft of my new book. Axed out of Luck: A Whodunit in the Woods pours out of me as if it's being dictated by someone else. Every sense I have tingles, and I know before it's even fully written that this is the book that is going to change everything.

———

ready for more hideaway at the lagoon?

Subscribe to my FREE newsletter and get a book sent straight to your inbox.

Shop directly with Elsie and save on the whole Hideaway at the Lagoon series.

Read Eloise's story in Daddy Vibes Lumberjack, Hideaway at the Lagoon Book Three.

about the author

I'm Elsie & I'm so happy you're here, you're going to fall in love tonight

I write short & steamy small-town romance stories about mountain men, lumberjacks, and ranchers. If you are looking to escape reality and fall into the arms of a man who will never let you down, you've come to the right place.

All of my books come with the promise of relatable characters, funny dialogue, no cheating, no cliffhangers & a happily ever after

You deserve to treat yourself to falling in love with your new book boyfriend!

Hugs,

Elsie James

Subscribe to my Newsletter and get a FREE EBook sent straight to your inbox!

Access exclusive deals when you shop directly with Elsie!

Grab more delicious Bonus Content when you join the Treat Team as a FREE member on Patreon!

💋 Learn more: https://elsiejamesauthor.com/